W9-CDG-094

BOOK 6

NANCY CLANCY

Soccer Mania

WRITTEN BY
Jane O'Connor

ILLUSTRATIONS BY
Robin Preiss Glasser

WITH
CAROLYN BRACKEN

HARPER
An Imprint of HarperCollins*Publishers*

To Coach Adam, Nora, Zoe,
and all the other Green Goblins of Brooklyn.
From your biggest cheerleader!

—J.O'C.

To Will and Alex—
who are great sports and great at sports!

—R.P.G.

 For information address HarperCollins Children's Books, a division of HarperCollins Publishers, 195 Broadway, New York, NY 10007.
www.harpercollinschildrens.com

Library of Congress Cataloging-in-Publication Data
O'Connor, Jane.
Soccer mania / by Jane O'Connor ; illustrations by Robin Preiss Glasser. — First edition.
pages cm. — (Nancy Clancy ; book 6)
Summary: As her third-grade class makes its selections for the "Graveyard of Boring Words" and learns about "superb synonyms," slow-footed Nancy enthusiastically plays on the soccer team, with the goal of just being mediocre, or maybe even a little better than average.
ISBN 978-0-06-226967-6 (hardback)
[1. Soccer—Fiction. 2. Vocabulary—Fiction. 3. Schools—Fiction.] I. Preiss-Glasser, Robin, illustrator. II. Title.
PZ7.O222Sns 2015 2015005622
[Fic]—dc23 CIP
AC

Typography by Jeanne L. Hogle
15 16 17 18 19 CG/RRDH 10 9 8 7 6 5 4 3
❖
First Edition

CONTENTS

CHAPTER 1
NANCY'S GOAL

Soccer practice had just ended.

"All I want is to be mediocre," Nancy told Bree. Mediocre meant being average, or in the middle. "That's not asking much. I'll never be great. But I hate being terrible." Nancy sighed. "Mediocre. That's my goal."

"You *are* mediocre," Bree assured her. Then she said in a whisper, "Clara is way worse than you. So is Yoko. So is Tamar. Well—" Bree stopped to think about that some more. "Actually, you and Tamar are tied." That was one of the superb things about Bree. Nancy could always count on her best friend to be completely honest.

"No, Bree," Grace butted in. "Nancy is worse than Tamar."

Nancy could always count on Grace to listen in on private conversations. It was like her ears had superpowers!

"Nancy, face it. You can't dribble. You don't have any control of the ball. And you get so scared whenever somebody kicks it to you. You're like—" Grace put her hands in front of her face and trembled as if she were watching a horror movie.

"And you're scared of falling. Look how clean you are!"

Grace's T-shirt and shorts were covered in grass stains. Nancy's were spotless.

Grace was right. But the way she pointed out stuff wasn't the same as how Bree did.

"You and I are tied for best on the team," Grace said to Bree. Their team was called the Green Goblins. "Then come Rhonda and Wanda. But neither of them can intercept like you."

Intercept meant getting the ball away

from a player on the other team. It was amazing, astounding, almost superhuman how speedy Bree was. Nancy's dad, who was their coach, called her Bolt. That was short for Lightning Bolt, because Bree could dribble fast with the ball and zigzag in between other players.

"I can't wait for our first game," Grace went on. It was on Saturday, only three days away. "Bree, you and I are going to rule!" Then they all reached into a bowl of oranges that were cut into quarters. Refreshments were Nancy's favorite part

of soccer. When Bree and Nancy finished sucking out the juice, they smiled wide-ly. The orange peels were still stuffed in their mouths.

"Hold it!" Nancy's dad said. He whipped out his smartphone for a photo.

Orange-peel smiles looked so absurd.

In the car on the way home, Nancy's dad said, "We're really coming together as a team. Bolt, love that fancy footwork! And Nancy, you are staying much more focused. During the scrimmage you always knew where the ball was."

"*Merci*," Bree and Nancy said at the same time.

Nancy's dad always had a compliment for her. She understood. He was trying to build up her confidence, but anybody, even the worst player in the world, could watch the ball. So Nancy said, "It's okay, Dad. I know I'm pretty bad." Then she told him the same thing she had told Bree before. "My goal is to become mediocre."

Bree and Nancy were in the backseat. Nancy could see her dad looking at her

through the car's rearview mirror. "No. No. Definitely wrong. Your goal is not to be mediocre. . . . Your goal is to score a goal." Then her dad cracked up at his own joke.

CHAPTER 2

ALMOST A SPORTS INJURY

"Come on. Let's do some more drills," Bree said as the car pulled into the Clancys' driveway. "We have time before it gets dark."

"Are you serious? I'm pooped." All Nancy wanted to do was collapse on the living room sofa. But Bree was out of the car and tugging Nancy by the arm.

"Practice makes perfect," Bree said. She said that about a lot of things—like tap-dancing, spelling, even learning pig Latin. Bree never settled for being mediocre at anything. She always wanted to be superb.

Nancy's dad heard Bree. "That's the spirit!" He opened the trunk of the car and tossed a soccer ball to Nancy.

"Okay, okay," Nancy muttered. Between her dad and Bree, it was two against one. She was outnumbered.

In the backyard, JoJo was pulling Freddy in her wagon. They were pretending to be on the way to a fire.

"Can you guys please play on the deck?" Bree asked. "Nancy and I need to practice soccer."

"No. We were here first," JoJo said.

"What if we let you play with us?" answered Bree.

"Big mistake!" Nancy told Bree at the same time JoJo and Freddy shouted, "Yes!" They ditched the wagon, took Frenchy into the house, and then listened to Bree explain some rules. Bree bent down on one knee with her hand on the ball, just the way Nancy's dad did while

talking to the team. It made Bree look very professional. “It’s not like catch. You can’t use your hands. All you can do is kick the ball.”

“I don’t like that rule,” Freddy said.

“Too bad,” Bree told her brother. “That’s how soccer is played.”

After they spread out, Bree said, “I’ll kick to Nancy and she’ll kick back to me. Then it’s your turn, JoJo. Freddy, you go third." Bree let out a whistle and passed the ball to Nancy. But before Nancy had a chance to return it, JoJo ran in front of her and kicked the ball—really hard for a little kid. Nancy watched it whiz back to Bree.

"Nice one, JoJo." Bree looked as surprised as Nancy was.

"Yay, me!" JoJo shouted, and jumped up and down. "Kick it again, Bree."

"It's supposed to be my turn," Nancy said sternly.

This time when Bree sent a fast ball skidding her way, Nancy managed to stop it with her foot and kick. Actually, it was more like a gentle tap. The ball rolled only a few feet away.

"Nice try!" Bree said. "You remembered to use the side of your foot, not your toes."

Actually Nancy hadn't done that on purpose. It just happened that way.

A little later, the twins—Rhonda and Wanda—showed up. They had missed practice because of a dentist appointment.

"Can we play?" Rhonda said. The twins were superb at all sports. Nancy was sure that one day they'd be in the Olympics and come home with loads of gold medals around their necks!

There were enough kids for a scrimmage. So everyone divided up—Bree, Wanda, and Freddy against Nancy, Rhonda, and JoJo.

"Freddy and JoJo, try to steal the ball away from the other side. And remember, use your feet. No hands." Then Bree let out another whistle.

Nancy ran her hardest. Soon she was gasping for air and had a pain in her side. Nobody else even seemed out of breath. At one point, JoJo stumbled over a ball that Nancy managed to stop. Nancy bent back her leg to kick when suddenly Freddy appeared out of nowhere and beat Nancy to

the ball. When her leg swung forward, all it connected with was air.

A second later Nancy lay sprawled on the ground. Bree and Wanda trotted over. "Are you hurt?"

Nancy examined her knee. It throbbed. Through the dirt, dots of red were appearing.

"Ooh!" Bree covered her eyes. She hated the sight of blood. It made her dizzy. She

looked the other way as she slung an arm around Nancy and helped her to the deck.

Nancy brushed grass and dirt off her T-shirt and shorts. Her clothes weren't spotless anymore. She watched everyone continue kicking the ball to one another. Even JoJo and Freddy were better than she was. And they were in preschool!

Soon it started to get dark. Everybody had to go home.

"*Au revoir.*" Nancy waved to her friends. That was French for "Good-bye."

As she limped upstairs, Nancy wondered if a banged-up knee counted as a sports injury. Maybe she wouldn't be able to play in the game on Saturday. Instead she could sit on the side and cheer for the Green Goblins. She'd pass out bottles of water and towels to players coming off the field. She'd wear her Goblins jersey and be in the team photo her dad took after the game. And win or lose, they'd go out for pizza at the King's Crown. All that would be really fun. Actually the only part of soccer that Nancy didn't enjoy so much was playing it.

That night, the mailbox bell rang. Nancy reeled in the basket that hung from a rope between her window and Bree's. In the basket were several pages of soccer tips. It was all the stuff Nancy's dad said at practices. Nancy never bothered to write any of it down, but Bree had.

Study these tips before the game, a note said in Bree's lovely handwriting.

1. Look for open spaces.
2. When in doubt, kick the ball out.
3. Don't kick the ball with your toes. Use the side of your foot.
4. Play hard and be tough but play fair.
5. No elbows!
6. Follow up and rebound.
7. Share the ball with other players. We're a team.

There was no time to study soccer now. Nancy had real homework to do for the Graveyard of Boring Words. So she stuffed the soccer tips in her desk drawer.

The Graveyard of Boring Words was something Nancy's teacher had thought up. Behind Mr. Dudeny's desk were a bunch of shoe boxes with cardboard tombstones. In each one were index cards with boring words on them. Words like "nice," "pretty," and "sad." On Halloween this year, instead of wearing different costumes, everyone in room 3D was coming as a ghost with boring words taped to their sheet.

For tomorrow Nancy had to think of three boring action words. An action word meant doing something, like walking or eating or singing. Then she had to come up with a Superb Synonym for each word. A synonym was a word that meant the same thing as the boring one.

She also had to put each of her Superb Synonyms in a sentence.

Rocking back in her desk chair, Nancy sat and pondered. That meant thinking really hard. She thought about playing soccer. Then she filled out three index cards.

Voilà! Nancy was done!

HERE LIES
BORING WORDS

CHAPTER 3

DRIBBLING

The next day in class practically everyone's hands shot up when Mr. Dudeny asked, "Who has some boring action words to share?" By the time the bell for recess rang, one of the shoe boxes was almost full. As each word got dropped into a tombstone, everybody shouted along with Mr. D, "BO-ring!"

Outside in the yard, Grace shouted to Bree, "Over here! I brought a soccer ball. We can practice."

Bree turned to Nancy. "Come on!"

Nancy shook her head. "You go. My knee still hurts." Instead she and Lionel hung on a low bar of the jungle gym and chatted. Lionel wasn't very good at sports either. In fact, he said that a fourth-grader

tried to pay him to stay off the boys' soccer team. "But my parents won't let me quit. They think being on a team builds character."

"My first soccer game is Saturday," Nancy said. "I'm frightened we'll lose 'cause of me."

Lionel understood and nodded. "Want me to come and cheer for you? What's your team's name?"

"The Green Goblins."

"Cool! I'll wear all green. I can be the team mascot."

"Really? That's so nice!" Nancy said, before remembering that "nice" was the very first boring word that had gone into a shoe box. She clapped a hand over her mouth as Lionel yelled, "BO-ring!"

In the distance Nancy could see Bree tap-tapping the soccer ball back and forth between her feet as she crossed the school yard. "Look at Bree. I wish I could dribble like that."

"Dribbling? That's easy. Watch!" Lionel slurped up a big mouthful of spit juice—the proper word was saliva—and let it trickle down his chin.

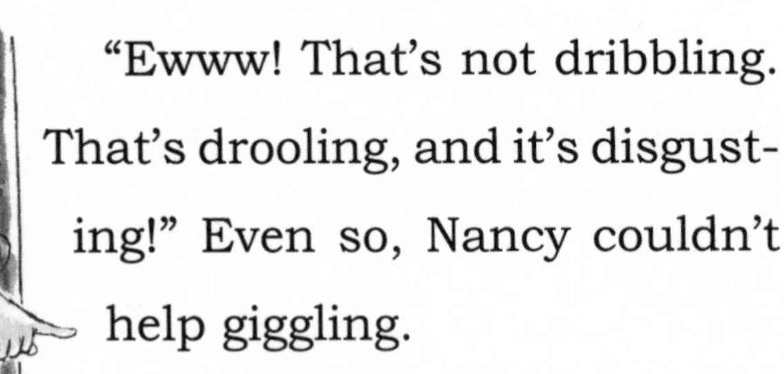

"Ewww! That's not dribbling. That's drooling, and it's disgusting!" Even so, Nancy couldn't help giggling.

Suddenly Lionel's eyes grew wide. "Bee alert!" he yelled, pointing at Nancy.

Sacre bleu! That was French for "Yipes!" Sure enough, a bee—a big fat one—was buzzing around Nancy's legs. It looked like it was coming in for the kill.

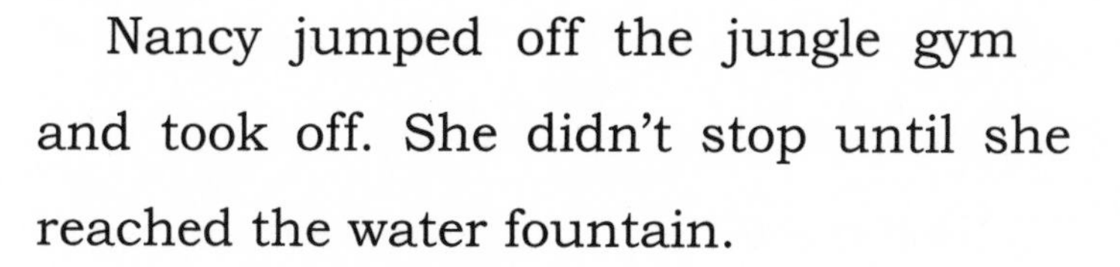

Nancy jumped off the jungle gym and took off. She didn't stop until she reached the water fountain.

The bee was gone.

Lionel caught up with her.

"*Merci*," Nancy said, out of breath. "That was a close call." Then she took a drink of water.

Just like how Bree was scared of blood, Nancy was scared of bees. She'd never been stung until last year. It happened at the second-grade family picnic. While she was eating ice cream, two bees attacked Nancy. Nobody else had gotten stung. It was as if she were a bee magnet. Beestings were even worse than shots!

Just then the bell rang. Recess was over. Before they headed inside, Lionel bent over the water fountain. When his cheeks were full, he turned to Nancy and let all the water in his mouth dribble down his face.

"You are such a goofball," Nancy said.

The front of Lionel's T-shirt was soaking wet. Lionel didn't care. If a joke got a laugh the first time, Lionel was positive it was even funnier the second time . . . and the third and the fourth and the fifth.

That afternoon Lionel came over to

Nancy's for their weekly checkers game. Lionel was a better player. But today he didn't notice that Nancy could triple-jump his kings. Nancy won.

"I have a surprise," Lionel told Nancy as they scooped up the checkers and put away the board.

"A surprise!" JoJo was riding her scooter in the hall and heard. "I want to see." She came into Nancy's room.

"Okay. It's going to take me a minute." Lionel left with his backpack. Nancy and JoJo heard the bathroom door shutting.

"What's he doing?" JoJo asked.

"I don't know. If I did, it wouldn't be a surprise."

A little bit later, Lionel reappeared. He had changed into green shorts and a green T-shirt from Otto's Auto Body Shop. Green makeup was smeared on his face. He was wearing a green Afro wig, plastic fangs with fake blood on them, and rubber gloves that looked like monster hands. Lionel held his arms out and walked stiffly, moaning, "*Gooooo*, Goblins!"

"JoJo, he's a green goblin!" Nancy cried. "Because that's the name of my soccer team."

JoJo didn't answer. Her face looked frozen. Then she clamped her eyes shut. Her mouth opened so wide, it looked like a big black hole. Out of it came a bloodcurdling scream.

"Don't be scared!" Nancy clasped her sister by the shoulders. "It's only Lionel."

Lionel removed his fangs. "Yeah! It's

just me!” He took off the monster hands and wig too. “Look!”

JoJo didn’t look. She broke away from Nancy and tore out of the room, still screaming.

“Wow, I didn’t expect that,” Lionel said to Nancy.

"JoJo gets scared really easily." A couple of weeks ago, Nancy, JoJo, Bree, and Freddy had been watching *Frozen.* When the giant snowman came on, JoJo got so scared, she wet her pants. Nancy didn't tell Lionel about that.

They found JoJo in Nancy's parents' bedroom.

"JoJo, I didn't mean to scare you. Honest," Lionel said.

"It's okay. JoJo understands that," Nancy's mom said. Then she stood and took JoJo by the hand. "Come on, missy. Let's get you in the tub. How about a bubble bath?"

A bath so early? Usually JoJo didn't take a bath until after dinner. And usually she put up a fuss. But not now. As her sister followed their mom into the bathroom, Nancy suddenly understood why. There was a big wet patch down JoJo's leggings.

Another accident! Nancy felt bad for her little sister. Fear could do terrible things to a person!

AWESOME
HERE LIES
HERE LIES
HERE LIES
BORING WORDS
BORING WORDS
R.I.P.
RAD

CHAPTER 4

J-J-JITTERS

On Friday everybody brought in more index cards. This time the cards had boring describing words on them. “Sad,” “pretty,” “mean,” “great,” and “bad” got dropped into one of the shoe boxes.

Mr. Dudeny held up an index card. “Here’s mine.” The word “awesome” was written on it.

"Wait a minute. That's not a boring word. It's long and hard to spell," Grace said. "'Great' is boring. 'Awesome' isn't."

Mr. Dudeny looked around the room. "Who agrees with Grace?"

A lot of hands went up, including Bree's.

"Okay. Now, who disagrees?" Mr. D asked. "And if so, tell me why 'awesome' belongs in the Graveyard."

Clara started to raise her hand.

"Yes, Clara," Mr. D said encouragingly.

"Um, sorry. Never mind. Actually I don't think it's a boring word either."

"Ooh, I think I know," Nancy said. "Mr. D, you told us a word gets boring if it is used too much. And all of us say 'awesome' all the time."

"Exactly."

"Awesome" joined the other boring words in the Graveyard. Everybody shouted, "BO-ring!"

After school, late that afternoon, there was another soccer practice.

The Green Goblins played their worst ever. Even Bree, Grace, and the twins goofed up big-time. Grace kept smacking her forehead whenever she made a mistake.

Everyone looked relieved when it started to rain and practice was cut short.

Before going home, Nancy's dad gathered the team in one of the Little League dugouts. "Okay, so you all have a case of the jitters. That's perfectly normal before a game."

"We stunk. We're going to get clobbered tomorrow."

"Grace, I don't want to hear negative talk like that," Nancy's dad said. He waited until Grace nodded to show she understood. "The Goblins are going to do great. It's like putting on a play. A bad dress rehearsal always means opening night will be wonderful."

Nancy started to worry that her father might bring up what he called his "career in showbiz." In college, he'd been a mime. That meant acting stuff out without talking. But all he said now was, "Get a good night's rest. Win or lose, I'm proud to be your coach. So . . ."

Everybody knew what to do next. They did a palm pileup, then threw up their hands and yelled, "Go, Goblins!"

During the car ride home, Nancy and Bree were quiet. An old rock song came on the radio.

"Hey, listen to the lyrics. This is called 'We Are the Champions.' It's by Queen. One of my all-time favorite groups."

As the song played, Nancy's dad sang along. He knew all the words.

At the traffic light, the car stopped. Nancy's father turned to the backseat. "You two look really stressed." When the light changed, he hung a left.

"Dad, this isn't the way home."

"So, does either of you know what 'stressed' spelled backward is?" he asked.

"No, Dad," Nancy said.

"Well, figure it out."

"D-E-S-S," Nancy started spelling slowly.

"Oh, I know!" Bree suddenly shouted. "'Stressed' backward is 'desserts'!"

Nancy's father parked less than a block from Cohen's Ice Cream Shoppe. He opened a big golf umbrella and held the car door open for Nancy and Bree. *"Après vous!"* That meant "After you!" in French.

Speaking French and treating them to ice cream. Double ooh la la! There couldn't be a more superb soccer coach on the planet!

Email messages Friday night

between Nancy and Lionel

Lionel: What time is the game? What's the name of the other team?

Nancy: It's at eleven. I don't know the team's name. They go to school in Pelham.

Lionel: I made up a cheer. And it has a big word in it just for you.

Two, four, six, eight!

Who will we annihilate? Pelham, Pelham, boo!

In case you don't know, annihilate means kill.

Nancy: *Merci!* But my dad won't like it. He's our coach and he only lets us do cheers that say nice things. Sorry!

Lionel: Will JoJo be there?

Nancy: No. She's going to Mrs. DeVine's.

Lionel: Then I'll look even scarier!

CHAPTER 5

EARLY-MORNING MANICURES

The next morning, Bree arrived at Nancy's house at the crack of dawn. She was already in her Goblins uniform.

"How come you're here so early?" Nancy asked. She was still in her nightie.

"My parents both have to go into work. They can't come to the game." Bree made

a face. "So I'm going with you." Then she held up a bottle of nail polish. "Look. My mom got me green nail polish."

"Ooh la la!"

"Green nail polish with sparkles," Bree added.

"Double ooh la la!"

"We have time for mani-pedis before the game," Bree went on. "I'll do you and you do me."

Half an hour later they were finished. Nancy fanned out her fingers and blew on them. "I swear you could work in a beauty salon," she told Bree. There were hardly any smears on Nancy's fingernails.

Bree was flapping her hands so her nails would dry faster. They both carefully pulled out the wads of Kleenex stuck between their toes. Nancy wiggled hers. It was superb the way her toenails sparkled.

Then she got out her shorts, her cleats, and special socks. They had green shamrocks all over. Shamrocks were Irish clover leaves. They were supposed to bring good luck. The last thing she put on was her jersey and—*voilà*—she was a Green Goblin. Normally, Nancy didn't like looking the same as everybody else. She liked to follow her own fashion sense. But wearing a team uniform—well, this was different.

Nancy and Bree stared at each other and made jazz hands.

"We look awe—" Nancy caught herself before saying "awesome." "We look outstanding!"

"Girls, are you ready to roll?" her father called upstairs.

"Oops! Almost forgot." Bree took out her earrings and put them on Nancy's dresser.

No one could wear earrings—it was a rule. That was one more thing Nancy liked about soccer. She didn't have to feel jealous that her ears weren't pierced yet.

Nancy took a last look at herself in the mirror. Wearing the Goblins jersey actually made her feel more athletic. She was nervous, but excited too. In the kitchen, they put on their cleats. As they clickety-clacked across the deck—cleats made almost the same sound as real tap shoes!—Nancy imagined kicking the ball hard. Up, up it would soar. The other team's goalie would jump for it but miss. It'd be a goal for the Green Goblins! Nancy realized that the chances of that happening were slim, which meant hardly at all. Still, you never knew.

CHAPTER 6

THE HORNETS ATTACK!

"They're who we have to play?" Nancy said, shocked. "Dad—I mean, Coach, those girls are giants!"

All twelve Goblins were huddled around Nancy's father. Everyone, even Grace, looked worried.

The other team was on the field

practicing. They wore black shorts and yellow jerseys. One girl was juggling a soccer ball with her feet. Another bounced a soccer ball from one knee to the other.

"They look like they're in middle school!" said Bree.

"They're not. The Hornets are in our league," Nancy dad said. "They're the same age you girls are."

"Did you say Hornets?" Nancy gulped. Hornets were like bees. She pictured a swarm of them attacking her.

"Just because the Hornets are big doesn't mean they're fast. You girls are swift." Her dad looked over at Bree, Tamar, and the twins. "Defenders, you have to stop the Hornets and pass the ball to midfielders. Midfielders, you have to move the ball to the attackers so they can score. Understand?"

Then her father went over what they'd been doing at practices. He stopped when the Hornets' coach came over and motioned to him.

A moment later Nancy's dad returned. "Okay. Here's the situation. The Hornets are short a player. Only eight girls showed up."

"Doesn't that mean they give up the game and we win?" Nola asked, excited.

Ooh la la! Nancy fist-bumped with Bree. Talk about an easy victory!

"Hold on, ladies.

Think about it. How would you feel if it was the other way around and we were down a player? So here's what we're going to do." Nancy's dad explained that during each quarter, someone from their team would play for the Hornets.

"Play against the Goblins! That's like fighting for the enemy!" Wanda exclaimed.

"Wait. Maybe it's not such a bad thing," Grace said to Wanda. "We can let them have Clara or Nancy."

Nancy's dad didn't hear, because he was already halfway to the cooler. When he came back he said, "I've got twelve straws. One is short. Whoever picks it will start out a Hornet."

It turned out to be Nancy.

Grace did a small fist pump.

“Thanks, girls. We really appreciate it,” the other coach said, and handed Nancy a yellow jersey. She pulled it on over her green one.

“I don’t like you being the enemy,” Clara said.

“Me too,” said Bree.

“Me three.” Wearing a yellow jersey

felt all wrong to Nancy. Wrong and hot. The game hadn't even started and already Nancy was perspiring.

"*Au revoir!*" she said sadly to the Goblins, and joined the other team.

The Hornets' coach was named Mrs. Fonda. She told Nancy that she'd be playing defense, when a car pulled to a stop. The back door opened.

Lionel had arrived.

When he found out why Nancy was wearing a yellow jersey, his fangs fell out of his mouth. "What?! You mean I'm here and I can't cheer for you?"

"It's only for ten minutes."

⚽ ⚽ ⚽

Nancy's dad was sadly mistaken about the Hornets. Not only were they big, they were speedy. The Goblins won the coin toss and chose to take the ball. But Yoko's first kick went straight to a Hornet.

After that, for almost the entire quarter, the soccer ball stayed within striking distance of the Goblins' goal. Only once did a Hornet kick it out of bounds. However, when Tamar took a throw-in and tossed the ball back toward Wanda, a Hornet jumped in for the ball, dribbled around Bree, and scored. Nancy kept running around after the ball, but it was

like she was invisible to the Hornets. They never passed to her.

By the time the whistle blew and the quarter ended, the score was still 1–0.

Nancy was dripping wet. "Sorry!" she said, handing over the soggy yellow jersey to Nola, who was playing next for the Hornets.

Nancy sat out for most of the second quarter. That was fine with her. She and Lionel did some cheers. "When you're out, you're out! When you're in, you're in!" they shouted to the crowd of parents sitting on the sidelines. "And when you're a Green Goblin, you win, win, win!"

Cheering didn't help. Almost right away a Hornet midfielder captured the ball from Grace and passed to an open striker, who took aim and scored. The score was now 2–0. Grace blinked and looked bewildered.

For the rest of the quarter, Grace's mother kept yelling, "Grace, hustle more! And watch out for number eight. You've

got eyes. Use them!" One time when Grace ran past, she said, "Mom, stop. I'm trying my best."

At the half, Nancy's dad passed out water bottles and towelettes. Everyone sat on the grass in the shade around him. "The Hornets are tough competitors. Really tough. I'm very proud of how you're staying scrappy and fighting for the ball. That's not easy on a hot day like this."

Her dad made the team rest during halftime. Everyone lay on their backs. Lionel too. He pretended to be dead. His tongue hung out and his eyes were rolled back so only the whites showed.

Right before the third quarter, Grace's mom pulled Grace off to the side. Nancy couldn't help overhearing.

"No, Grace. They are not all great players. Number three kicks wildly," Grace's mother was saying. "Do you realize you

missed a chance to score? You had the ball. Why on earth did you pass to Clara? She's the worst on the team!"

"Lookit. Our coach wants us to pass if somebody is wide open."

"Oh, really? Well, I bet he also wants you to win. And that's not going to happen. Not the way you're playing."

Grace nodded and kept her eyes on the ground.

During the second half, Nancy started out as a defender. But she was switched to midfield after the same Hornet striker got by her a few times. Nancy hated midfield. It meant running back and forth without stopping. She was always behind the pack of players. If only she wasn't cursed with slow legs!

At the end of the third quarter, Bree sneaked past the Hornets' defense. She dribbled down the field. Nobody was covering Rhonda, and Bree kicked a soft one to her. It looked as if Rhonda's kick was going left. So that's where the

Hornets' goalie went. But the ball skidded to the right and hit the net before the goalie could grab it.

A goal for the Goblins! Now the score was 2–1.

Her dad was screaming "Woo-hoo!" at the top of his lungs and high-fived Lionel.

During the fourth quarter, twice Grace jumped in front of Nancy and took control of the ball. Grace was being a ball hog. But maybe she'd get another goal and tie the score.

Nancy watched Grace dribble the ball in the direction of the Goblins' goal. The field was pretty clear.

Grace kept the ball under control and headed nearer the goal.

"You can nail it, Gracie!" her mother yelled.

All the Goblin parents were up on their feet now and cheering. Lionel too.

Grace kept dribbling toward the goal. Hornets defenders were gaining on her. She was still much too far away to score. She looked around. Bree was just in front and open. Grace passed to her.

That was a mistake. A huge, gigantic, enormous mistake.

Bree was a Hornet for the fourth quarter.

A second too late, Grace realized what she'd done.

Bree had no choice but to dribble the

other way down the field. She passed to an open Hornet, who slammed the ball to another girl in yellow.

Whoosh! The kick was high and hard. Nancy watched the soccer ball fly past Yoko, the Goblins' goalie. It was a dream kick. Exactly the kind Nancy had imagined doing.

The score was now 3–1 and stayed that way until the ref blew the final whistle. Game over.

It was hard to tell who felt worse, Grace or Bree.

"I forgot Bree was a Hornet. Even with a yellow shirt on, I forgot!"

"I hated helping the Hornets win." Bree had a hand over her eyes and shook her head. They both kept saying sorry to the other Goblins, even though Nancy's father said there was no need to apologize. "Mistakes happen. That's sports. You guys were cooking the last quarter. We're talking one goal and some smart plays against a fierce team of high school girls."

"Wait—you said they were our age."

“My dad’s joking to make us feel better,” Nancy explained to Clara.

“And now, if my watch is correct”—Nancy’s father glanced at his wrist—“the King’s Crown should be open for business.”

⚽ ⚽ ⚽

Two medium pizzas later, everyone felt much better. Lionel came too. He claimed that his root beer was making him drunk. He kept burping and falling off his chair until Nancy’s dad told him to cool it. Nancy reeled in a long string of melted cheese with her tongue. There was nothing like pizza to make you forget about the agony of defeat.

fish +

CHAPTER 7
CHEERLEADING

Lionel's first soccer game was tomorrow. Bree and Nancy decided to go root for him.

"What's the name of his team?" Bree wanted to know.

"The Dolphins."

"Hmm. That's a problem." Bree pooched

out her lips. "How are we going to be team mascots?"

"We can't. There's no way we can make ourselves look like dolphins. Let's go as cheerleaders!"

They high-fived each other.

Nancy emailed Lionel.

Nancy: What color are your team shirts?

Lionel: Blue. Why?

Nancy: Bree and I are coming to cheer for you.

Lionel: I stink. Don't bother coming.

Lionel's email wasn't going to stop Bree or Nancy. Nancy was sure—almost 100 percent positive—that they would bring Lionel good luck.

They got busy figuring out what to wear:

Blue tank tops

Blue tutus

Blue hair ribbons

Blue sneakers

The sparkly green polish on their fingernails clashed with their outfits. So they gave themselves new manicures.

"Singin' the Blues" was the color they chose.

Then they went next door for Saturday tea with Mrs. DeVine. Their neighbor, they learned, had been a cheerleader herself in days of yore. "I bet my pom-poms are somewhere in the attic."

Nancy and Bree helped search. Sure enough, in a dusty carton marked *High School*, Mrs. DeVine found what she was looking for. Underneath a white sweater with a big letter *C* on it and a short red skirt were pom-poms with gorgeous silver streamers.

"You may have them," said Mrs.

DeVine, handing one pair to Bree and another to Nancy.

"For real?" Bree gasped.

"I can't imagine I'll be using them anytime soon."

Nancy hugged Mrs. DeVine. *"Merci! Merci mille fois."* That meant "A thousand thanks!"

"We're going to cheer for our friend Lionel tomorrow. At his soccer game."

"Oh, yes. Lionel." Mrs. DeVine pursed her lips and sniffed. Lionel was not one of her favorite people. The one time Nancy had brought him over for tea, he kept speaking in a fake British accent. It had gotten on Mrs. DeVine's nerves.

Later that afternoon Nancy and Bree practiced shaking the pom-poms in time to their leaps and scissor kicks. It got very chilly. Their teeth were chattering as they yelled out cheers.

Finally Bree's mother insisted they put on jackets or come inside. Jackets spoiled the cheerleading look. So after Bree did one more split—another thing she had practiced to perfection—they said *au revoir* and hoped for warm weather tomorrow.

DOLPHIN

CHAPTER 8

ANOTHER SPORTS INJURY

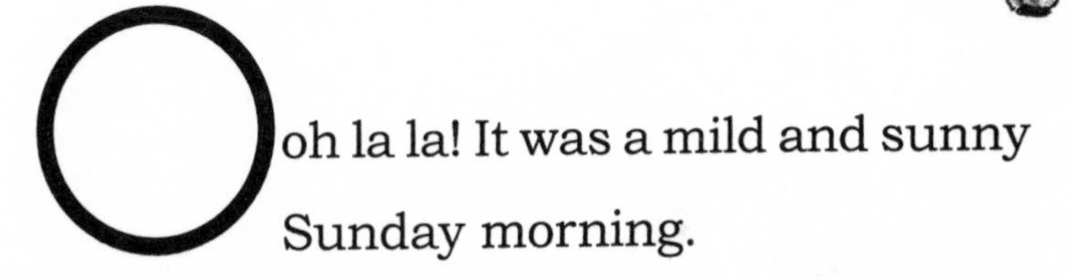

Ooh la la! It was a mild and sunny Sunday morning.

Bree and Nancy had no trouble spotting Lionel. He was the shortest on the team. His Dolphins shirt was way too big on him. His face was a pale, sickly green.

"Not all the face paint came off," he

explained. “I told the coach I was sick and might puke. But he didn’t fall for it. He’s making me play.”

“We’re going to bring you good luck!” Nancy said. “Just wait and see.”

“I don’t need luck. I need a miracle.”

Bree crossed her arms and looked stern. “Oh, no! That is exactly the wrong attitude.” Then she said, “To be a winner, think like a winner. That’s what our coach always tells us. Isn’t that right, Nancy?”

Nancy nodded.

Then they did a cheer expressly for Lionel. That meant it was just for him. Nancy had made it up last night.

“He tells jokes like no one can. But we’re not joking—Lionel’s the man!”

Shaking their pom-poms, they leaped in the air.

"You guys are the best—no joke," Lionel said. Then he joined the Dolphins and their coach. As he walked off, he looked like a prisoner going to his doom. His Dolphins shirt hung down so low, it looked like a dress!

Five minutes later the game started.

Watching Lionel play was painful. There was no other way to describe it. The only time he captured the ball was when he caught it—in his arms.

Then, in the final minutes of the game, with the Dolphins behind 5–3, something really and truly painful happened.

Lionel was playing midfield after sitting out all of the second and third quarters. He was running after the ball. He didn't see a big kid from the other team barreling toward him from the side of the field. The other kid was signaling for the ball. He didn't see Lionel.

Wham! They slammed into each other. Lionel fell backward and landed with his leg twisted in a weird way.

"Ooooh!" Both sides of the field gasped.

"This looks bad!" Nancy whispered.

Bree had both hands clapped over her mouth. Her eyes were squinched shut. "I can't look. Tell me what's going on."

Nancy started reporting. "Lionel can't get up. Both coaches are running over to him. His mom too. The kid who banged into him is okay. But he looks really upset." Nancy paused. The coaches were lifting up Lionel. "Okay. The coaches are carrying Lionel off the field now. They've got him under his arms. You can look. I don't see blood."

Bree cracked open her eyes a tiny bit.

They watched Lionel pass by and

waved their pom-poms at him. He managed to wave back. His face looked even greener now.

Nancy and Bree led the Dolphins in a cheer.

"Gimme an *L*, gimme an *I*, gimme an *O*, gimme an *N*—"

They didn't get to finish spelling Lionel's name before his mom's car sped off. It was all very dramatic—like a scene out of a movie.

Back at Bree's that afternoon, they called Lionel several times and left voice messages.

Finally around four o'clock, he called. "I didn't break anything. It's just a really bad sprain. My mother took me to a bone specialist."

"A what?" Nancy and Bree both asked at the same time.

"A doctor who knows all about bones. The guy is friends with my parents. His patients are all famous athletes."

Ooh la la! That was glamorous.

"I have crutches."

Double ooh la la!

"I feel terrible," Bree said. "We didn't bring good luck. We brought bad luck."

"No. You're wrong. You did bring good luck. I can't play for the rest of the soccer season!"

FINISH

CHAPTER 9

ALMOST HALLOWEEN

Lionel hobbled around on crutches for a whole month.

At recess kids raced against him with two legs tied together. Like in a three-legged race. Lionel sometimes beat them. "I've never won a race before—ever!" he'd say proudly. "I'm a much better athlete on crutches."

Throughout October Lionel arrived every Saturday for the Green Goblins games. The Goblins lost all of them.

At the last game, Grace's mother joined the halftime huddle and told the Goblins what they were doing wrong. She kept butting in while Nancy's dad was talking. Finally, her father said, "Thanks for the tips. But I think it's confusing for the girls to hear two of us."

Grace was glaring at her mom.

When the game was over, Nancy overheard Grace's mother saying, "There is no excuse for the way you played today."

"Mom, you make me nervous when you run down the field screaming while I'm trying to play!"

Grace didn't come to the King's Crown afterward. So there was pizza left over. Nancy's father had brought it home, and now it was wrapped in foil in the fridge.

Around four o'clock Nancy decided a slice of pepperoni was just the thing to give her extra brainpower. She needed it. She was suffering from writer's block. That meant she was stuck trying to come up with an idea for a short story. For Monday she had to write one with lots of Superb Synonyms.

After heating up a slice of pizza in the microwave, Nancy sat in the kitchen and pondered. She wanted her story to star Lucette Fromage. She was a nine-year-old girl Nancy had made up. Lucette had many superb adventures.

Nancy's mom joined her at the kitchen table. She had her laptop out and was searching for costume ideas for JoJo. Halloween was only a week away.

"What about a deep-sea diver?" Nancy suggested. JoJo and Freddy were always going around in goggles and flippers pretending to search for treasure.

"I suggested that. But Freddy is going as a deep-sea diver. JoJo wants to be different. So far everything I suggest is either too babyish or too scary." Her mother kept her eyes on the laptop screen. "She's not even sure she wants to go trick-or-treating. She's worried other kids will look too scary."

Nancy folded over her pizza and let some grease dribble onto her plate. "How come JoJo's such a fraidycat all of a sudden?"

"Oh, it's just a stage she's going through. It will pass."

JoJo appeared at that very moment.

She hopped on their mother's lap while Mom continued to look for costume ideas. JoJo shook her head at every suggestion.

Princess? No.

Puppy? No.

Dinosaur? Definitely no.

All of a sudden, before she could take back the words, Nancy said, "Want to be a cheerleader with Bree and me?"

"Yes! Yes! Yes!" JoJo jumped off Mom's lap and threw her arms around Nancy.

"Stop!" Nancy pushed her sister away.

"You're getting pizza grease on me!"

"I'm telling Freddy! Right now!" JoJo zipped out of the kitchen.

Her mother closed the laptop. "Without a doubt, you are the best sister ever."

"No, Mom. 'Best' is a boring word. I am the most spectacular sister ever!"

The pizza worked. Almost as soon as she took the last bite, a story idea popped into Nancy's head. It was going to be about soccer, and since it was almost Halloween, she'd make it a spooky soccer story.

On a bookshelf in the living room

Nancy found the thesaurus. It was a special kind of dictionary—there was one in 3D's classroom too. You could look up any word in the thesaurus to find words that meant the same thing. Whoever invented the thesaurus was a genius!

The Bewitched Soccer Ball, Nancy wrote at the top of the paper. She made sure the story was loaded with Superb Synonyms. There was one in almost every sentence!

Lucette Fromage was the most superlative runner on the Scarlet Robins.

She expected the team to triumph today. But every time she attempted to dribble, the ball stopped all on its own and rolled away. It was spooky. It was eerie. It was supernatural! Had someone on the opposing team cast a spell on it? Oui, oui, oui. That was exactly what had occurred.

Superlative—best

Scarlet—red

Triumph—win

Attempt—try

Eerie, supernatural—scary

Occur—happen

An hour later Nancy was done. Lucette figured out who was bewitching the ball. Lucette first told the girl to stop being a bad sport. When that didn't work, Lucette bribed her with some candy and the girl un-bewitched the soccer ball.

Not only was the story entertaining, it was almost two pages long. It ended with Lucette scoring the winning goal—a header—for her team. Nancy made a cover for her story. On it the soccer ball was boinging off Lucette Fromage's head. Nancy loved creative writing because you could make everything work out exactly the way you wished it would in real life.

The next week whizzed by. Soccer practice got canceled both times. Once because of rain and once because Nancy's dad had to work late. Nancy and Bree made up for lost time by doing drills in the backyard.

During recess everyone on the Green Goblins practiced too.

"You really are improving," Bree said after Nancy kicked a ball past her to Wanda.

"You think?" Nancy was trying her best. Each night, after her homework was done, Nancy even went over the soccer tips from Bree.

"Oh yes," Rhonda agreed. "You're running faster. You don't look all—" Rhonda started flapping her arms and legs as if she were a rag doll.

Since Halloween fell on a Saturday this year, Ada M. Draezel Elementary School was celebrating it on Friday.

The day before, the kids in 3D decorated their classroom. A sign on the door said,

Enter if you dare! Ghosts made out of paper chains hung from the ceiling. Fake cobwebs covered Mr. Dudeny's desk, the bookshelves, and the windows. A lot of the cobweb stuff was left over. So Lionel wrapped himself in it, and *voilà*, he was a mummy. But by the end of the day he had pretty much uraveled.

Before the last bell, everybody took home a few index cards from the tombstone shoe boxes. The kids were supposed to tape them on their ghost costumes. Nancy had "nice," "bad," and "excited."

Bree had “sad,” “pretty,” and “awesome,” which she still didn’t think should count.

Right after lunch on Friday, the ghosts of 3D got to parade through the hallways moaning the boring words taped on their sheets. There were flowery ghosts, striped ghosts, and polka-dotted ghosts. It turned out nobody’s family used white sheets anymore.

"I don't think we look very scary," a ghost whispered in Clara's voice. The ghost was wearing a Sesame Street sheet.

"Same here." Nancy had on an old Strawberry Shortcake sheet. *Have berry sweet dreams!* was printed all over it. "This was the only one my mom let me have." Then she continued moaning. "'Nice' . . . 'Bad' . . . 'Excited.'"

It turned out there were a ton of Superb Synonyms for "excited." And it was interesting how that one word could mean such different things. You could be excited in a happy way. The word for that was "thrilled." Or you could be excited in a nervous way. The word for that was "anxious."

By Saturday evening Nancy was both

thrilled and anxious. She was thrilled because it was Halloween. She was anxious because the last game of the season was only seventeen hours away.

Nancy returned from trick-or-treating with a pillowcase full of candy. She and Bree held a weigh-in. Ooh la la! They each had hauled in more than two pounds!

Right before Bree went home, they traded. Nancy gave Bree her Reese's Peanut Butter Cups and red licorice in exchange for all of Bree's mini Snickers and Tootsie Pops. Yet Nancy found that she couldn't eat much candy. Thinking about the final game made her lose her appetite. And that night she had insomnia. It took her ages to fall asleep.

It seemed like only a minute later that

her mom was telling her to get up and get ready.

Downstairs in the kitchen, JoJo was back in her Halloween costume. "I'm going to cheer for you."

"*Merci!*" Nancy said sleepily. "But remember, Lionel will be there. He is not really a goblin. It's only Lionel."

After breakfast, Nancy went and found her pom-poms. She handed them to JoJo. "Here. You can borrow these."

JoJo shook the pom-poms and shouted, "Yay, me!" as the Clancys piled into the car.

CHAPTER 10

SEASON FINALE

It was the Green Goblins versus the Silver Streaks. The last game. The season finale.

"Oh boy! I know some of those girls from our travel team," Rhonda said. "They're good."

"As in great," Wanda added. "See that

girl with the red hair? Number eight. She can even do behind-the-back dribbles!"

"That's not a problem," Nancy's dad said. He had everyone gathered in a huddle. "When we're playing against a good team, what happens?"

"We play better!" Bree said.

"Exactly!" Nancy's father said.

Well . . . not exactly.

In the first quarter the Silver Streaks scored. Twice.

Nancy was goalie. The first time, the ball hit the net before she even realized a striker had kicked it. The second time, the ball zoomed way over Nancy's head.

As Nancy came off the field, JoJo was jumping up and down. "Yippee! Yippee!" she yelled.

“JoJo, you cheer when *we* score, not them,” Nancy explained. Then she turned to Bree. “All that practicing—I thought I was getting better. Almost mediocre. But I still stink.”

“Nobody could have stopped that last goal—except maybe a giant.”

Nancy sat out the second quarter next to Lionel. They shared some of his Hallow-een candy until bees arrived and circled

around Nancy's head. She swatted them with a towel. Bees! How could there still be bees? It was November!

The second quarter went no better than the first. Well, it did go a little better. The Silver Streaks only scored one goal, not two.

At halftime the score was 3–0. Nancy's dad gathered the team around him.

"I know what you're going to tell us," Grace said. She was sucking an orange slice and sounded bored. "You're going to say the score isn't important."

"That's right. It isn't." Nancy's father reminded the Goblins that there were two quarters left in the game. "We are going to play hard and finish the season the way we started. As a team." Then he made everybody do a palm pileup and shout, "Go, Goblins!"

The third quarter began and—lo and behold!—the Silver Streaks started making mistakes. Nancy was playing midfield. A player didn't notice where the last defender on her team was. Instead of slowing down, she sped up.

“Off sides!” The ref blew his whistle.

Tamar took the ball for the free kick. No one was defending Bree. Tamar passed to Wanda, who passed to Bree for a kick that the Silver Streaks’ goalie missed.

The Goblins scored!

“Way to go, Bolt!” Nancy’s dad screamed.

“Gimme a *B*, gimme an *R* . . . ,” Lionel started cheering.

Nancy wanted to run over and high-five Bree. But the Streaks were already in position and ready to kick off again. A Streaks player sent the ball soaring in an arc high in the air. Nancy watched as it rose up, up, up before it started to drop.

Sacre bleu! The ball was heading right for Nancy! A Streaks defender nearby moved in closer to her.

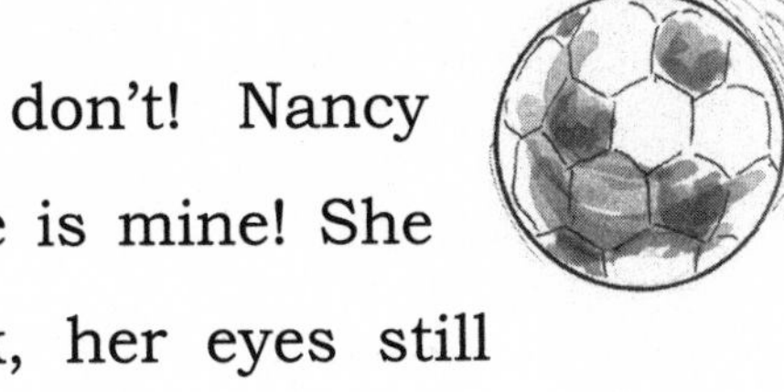

Oh, no, you don't! Nancy thought. This one is mine! She took a step back, her eyes still locked on the ball.

And then . . .

GREE
GOBLI

CHAPTER 11

TWO MORE SPORTS INJURIES

And then Nancy panicked.

A bee—a big, fat, hungry-looking one—was buzzing toward her!

She forgot about the soccer ball flying at her. She crouched down and covered her head.

Too late! The bee zapped her in the

neck. Nancy shot up from the pain.

Zwock! She got zapped again. This time in the face.

Was it another bee?

No! It was the soccer ball. It smacked her in the nose. Hard.

The next thing Nancy knew she was lying facedown on the ground.

“Medical emergency!” she heard Lionel yelling.

In a flash her father was beside her. Lots of Goblins too.

"Are you okay?" her dad was asking.

"I think so." Nancy rolled over. She kept her hands cupped over her nose. *Sacre bleu!* Did it hurt!

"We just scored!" Bree told her. "After you stopped the ball."

"With your face," Grace added. "And then *I* scored."

Nancy sat up. Her upper lip felt wet and sticky so she wiped it with the back of her hand. "You mean the score is now three to two?"

Bree did not reply. She was staring at Nancy's face. All of a sudden Bree's eyeballs rolled back in her head and her legs got wobbly.

"Timber!" Lionel shouted as Bree fell to the ground.

After Bree came to, her parents wanted to take her home. But she refused. "No way am I leaving before this game ends."

She and Nancy were sitting in beach chairs that Nancy's mom had brought. There were umbrellas attached to the arms.

Nancy's nose stopped gushing blood once her mother put ice on the back of her neck. That also made the bee sting feel better.

"I can't believe I fainted!" Bree kept saying. She held a wet towel pressed to her forehead. "Was it like in a movie? Was it very dramatic?" Then suddenly she stopped talking. "Oh, look! Clara just kicked a nice ball."

"Clara?"

"Yes, and Wanda's got it. She's heading downfield!"

Nancy and Bree both jumped out of the beach chairs to watch the action.

A couple of the Silver Streaks tried to overpower Wanda and steal the ball away. But she was too fast for them. Down the field she charged. When she saw that Rhonda was open, she side-kicked to her. Rhonda took control of the ball. Tap, tap, tap, she dribbled the ball from foot to foot. She was way past the center line now. Wanda was running right beside her. As soon as she got a little bit ahead, Rhonda whizzed the ball over to her.

"Go, Double Trouble!" Nancy's dad was screaming. "You can do it!"

Now all the Goblins parents were on their feet, cheering.

Wanda was no more than ten feet away from the Streaks' goal. Streaks defenders were gaining on her.

"Take your shot!" Nancy's dad yelled. "Kick that sucker now!"

Wanda did. It was a hard, fast kick.

The ball rocketed toward the net.

The Silver Streaks' goalie dove for it.

"Did she catch it?" Nancy clutched Bree's arm.

"I can't tell!"

The goalie rolled over. Her hands were empty!

The ball bounced against the back of the net as the final whistle blew.

The game ended in a 3–3 tie!

Bree and Nancy rushed onto the field with all the Goblins. Everybody was screaming, Nancy's dad the loudest.

"Whoooooo! We did it!" Her father's face was turning bright red. Scarlet. He flung himself on the ground, kicking and screaming for joy. Then he sprang up and led the team in a wild cha-cha line. "Go, go, Goblins," he chanted over and over. As he passed by Nancy's mother he pulled her into the cha-cha line. JoJo too.

"Okay, Doug," Nancy's mother said, laughing, when he finally stopped dancing. "Are you ready to calm down now?"

"Claire, didn't you see what just happened?"

"Yes. Yes. I saw. A tie. It was great!"

"'A tie'? That's all you can say?" Nancy's dad planted his hands on his hips. "Oh, *noooo*, Mrs. Clancy. This was way more than an ordinary tie. You just witnessed a great moment in sports—" Nancy's dad turned to the Goblins and gave two thumbs-up. "This was an against-the-odds, final-second, come-from-behind tie!" Then Nancy's dad called

to the parents, "Photo op!" while everybody on the team formed a pyramid.

Clara was smallest, so she was on top.

Nancy was in the bottom row next to Grace.

"Hey, I meant to say thanks," Grace said. "'Cause of you, I scored."

"Well, you're welcome. But it was an accident. I was trying to get away from a bee."

"Still, it happened. So it counts." Grace paused. She seemed to be pondering. "You're not such a rotten player anymore. You're almost average."

"You mean mediocre?"

"Yeah, I guess."

"*Merci*, Grace!" How many times before had Grace given Nancy a compliment? Like never.

Then they both stopped talking and smiled for the cameras.

Season over!